Marx
Joyce
Defoe Abbott Hardy Machiavelli Chesterton Emerson Austen
Melville Montaigne Cooper Hugo Grimm
Carroll Haggard Eliot
Stoker Christie Molière
Wilde Maupassant Byron Schiller
Garnett Engels Smith Kafka
Goethe Fitzgerald Hawthorne Hall
Cotton Einstein Dostoyevsky Willis
Baum Henry Kipling Doyle
Leslie Dumas Nietzsche
Flaubert Turgenev Balzac
Stockton Vatsyayana Crane
Burroughs Verne
Curtis Tocqueville Gogol Vinci
Homer Widger Tolstoy Whitman Busch
Darwin Thoreau Twain Scott
Potter Freud Zola Lawrence Plato Harte
Kant Jowett Stevenson Dickens Hesse
Andersen Burton
London Descartes Cervantes
Poe Aristotle Wells Voltaire Cooke
Hale James Hastings Burton
Bunner Shakespeare Irving
Richter Chambers
Doré da Shaw Benedict Alcott
Chekhov Pushkin
Dante Wodehouse Newton
Swift

tredition®

 Project Gutenberg

Poems

Matilda Betham

Imprint

This book is part of TREDITION CLASSICS

Author: Matilda Betham
Cover design: Buchgut, Berlin – Germany

Publisher: tredition GmbH, Hamburg - Germany
ISBN: 978-3-8424-7324-9

www.tredition.com
www.tredition.de

TO

LADY ROUSE BOUGHTON,
AS A TESTIMONY OF RESPECT AND
GRATITUDE FOR LONG CONTINUED
FRIENDSHIP,

THIS LITTLE VOLUME IS INSCRIBED BY
HER OBLIGED HUMBLE SERVANT, MATIL-
DA BETHAM.

ADVERTISEMENT.

Before this book was printed, I thoughtlessly concluded there must be a preface; but, on consideration, see no particular purpose it would answer, and gladly decline a task I should have undertaken with much timidity and reluctance. All I feel necessary to premise, is, that the tale in the Old Shepherd's Recollections is founded on an event which happened in Ireland; and that last spring I suppressed the song ending in page 65 [The Old Man's Farewell], some time after it had been in the hands of the composer, from meeting accidentally with a quotation in a magazine that resembled it.

CONTENTS.

POEMS.

THE OLD FISHERMAN.

'My bosom is chill'd with the cold,

My limbs their lost vigour deplore!

Alas! to the lonely and old,

Hope warbles her promise no more!

'Worn out with the length of my way,

I must rest me awhile on the beach,

To feel the salt dash of the spray,

If haply so far it may reach.

'As the white-foaming billows arise,

I reflect on the days that are past,

When the pride of my strength could despise

The keen-driving force of the blast.

'Though the heavens might menace on high,

I would still push my vessel from shore;

At my calling undauntedly ply,

And sing as I handled the oar.

'When fortune rewarded my toil,

And my nets, deeply-laden, I drew,

I hurried me home with the spoil,

And its inmates rejoic'd at the view.

'Though the winds and the waves were perverse,

I was sure to be welcom'd with glee;

My presence the cares would disperse,

That were only awaken'd for me.

'Whether weary, with toiling in vain,

Or gay, from abundant success,
I heard the same blessing again, —
I met the same tender caress:
'I fancied the perils repay'd,
That could such affection ensure;
By fondness and gratitude sway'd,
I was eager to dare and endure.
'My cot did each comfort contain,
And that gave my bosom delight;
When drench'd by the winterly rain,
I watch'd in my vessel at night.
'But, alas! from the tyrant, Disease,
What love or what caution can save!
A fever, more harsh than the seas,
Consign'd my poor wife to the grave.
'My children, so tenderly rear'd,
And pining for want of her care,
Though more by my sorrows endear'd,
Could not rescue my heart from despair.
'I tempted the dangers of night,
And still labour'd hard at the oar,
My sufferings appear'd to be light,
But I suffer'd with pleasure no more.
'And yet, when some seasons had roll'd,
I seem'd to awaken anew;
My children I lov'd to behold,
How tall and how comely they grew.
'My boy became hardy and bold,

His spirit was buoyant and free;

And, as I grew thoughtful and old,

Was loud and oppressive to me.

'But the girl, like a bird in the bower,

Awaken'd my hope and my pride;

She won on my heart ev'ry hour,

And I could not the preference hide.

'I mark'd the address and the care,

The manner endearing and mild,

Not dreaming those qualities rare

Were to murther the peace of my child:

'That grandeur would ever descend

To seek for so lowly a bride,

Or his fair one, a lover pretend,

From all she held dear to divide:

'That beauty was priz'd like a gem,

Expected to dazzle and shine,

Whose value the world would contemn,

Unless trac'd to some Indian mine:

'Alas! hapless girl! had I known

Thou hadst learnt to repine at thy lot;

That splendour and rank were thy own,

Thy home and thy father forgot:

'That lore and ambition assail'd,

Thou hadst left us, whatever befel!

My pardon and prayers had prevail'd,

I had blest thee, and bade thee farewel!

'With thy husband, from this happy clime,

I had seen thee for ever depart!
Still hoping affection and time
Might soften the pride of his heart:
'That a moment perhaps would arise,
When, fondling a child on the knee,
He might read, in its innocent eyes
A lesson of pity for me.
'But lips, which till then never said
A word to cause any one pain,
Inform'd me, when reason had fled,
Of a conflict it could not sustain.
'And he, who had wish'd to conceal
That the woman he lov'd had been poor,
Began all his folly to feel,
When the victim could hearken no more.
'Yet still for himself did he mourn,
And, indignant, I fled from the view:
For my wrongs were not easily borne,
And my anger was hard to subdue.
'One prop, one sole comfort, remain'd,
Who saw me o'erladen with grief,
Who saw (though I never complain'd)
My heart was too sick for relief.
'One, who always attentive and dear,
Every effort exerted to please,
My desolate prospect to cheer,
To study my health and my ease.
'For his was each toil and each care,

The due observations to keep;

To sit watching amid the night air,

And fancy his father asleep.

'Yet, dejected, and sadly forlorn,

I dar'd in my heart to repine, —

To lament that I ever was born,

Though such worth and affection were mine.

'Alas! I was destin'd to know,

However intense my despair,

I still was reserv'd for a blow,

More painful and cruel to bear.

'Yes! this only one fell in the main!

—I eagerly struggled to save;

But I strove with the current in vain,

And saw him sink under the wave!

'My head was astounded and wild, —

Incessant I roam'd on the shore,

To seek the dead corse of my child,

And to weep on his bosom once more.

'Seven days undisturb'd was the sky,

The eighth was a tempest most drear,

I saw the huge billow rise high!

I saw my lost treasure appear!

'Like a dream it seem'd passing away: —

I hurried me onward to meet,

And clasp the inanimate clay,

When senseless I sunk at his feet.

'These hands, now enfeebled by time,

The last pious offices paid!

Age sorrow'd o'er youth in its prime,

And my boy near his mother was laid.

'Now scar'd by the griefs I have known,

Wounds, apathy only can heal,

My joys and my sorrows are flown,

For I have forgotten to feel.

'But I know my Creator is just,

That his hand will deliver me soon;

I have learnt to submit and to trust,

Though I finish my journey alone.'

Aldborough, September 7, 1800.

LINES TO MRS. RADCLIFFE,

ON FIRST READING THE MYSTERIES OF UDOLPHO.

Enchantress! whose transcendant pow'rs,

With ease, the massy fabric raise; —

Beneath whose sway the tempest low'rs,

Or lucid stream mednd'ring plays; —

Accept the tribute of a heart,

Which thou hast often made to glow

With transport, oft with terror start,

Or sink at strains of solemn woe!

Invention, like a falcon, tam'd

By some expert and daring hand,

For pride, for strength and fierceness fam'd,

Implicit yields to thy command.

Now mounts aloft in soaring flight,
Shoots, like a star, beyond the sight;
Or, in capricious windings borne,
Mocks our faint hopes of safe return;
Delights in trackless paths to roam,
But hears thy call, and hurries home;
Checks his bold wing when tow'ring free,
And sails, without a pause, to thee!
Enchantress, thy behests declare!
And what thy strong delusions are!
When spirits in thy circle rise,
Gaunt Wonder, panic-struck, and pale,
Impatient Hope, and dread Surmise,
Attendants on the mystic tale!
How is it, with such vivid hues,
A harmonizing softness flows!
What are the charms that can diffuse,
Such grandeur as thy pencil throws!
Say! do the nymphs of classic lore,
So simply graceful, light, and fair,
Forsake their consecrated shore,
Their hallow'd groves, and purer air?
Tir'd of the ancient Grecian loom,
And smit with Fancy's wayward glance,
Weave they amid the Gothic gloom,
The high-wrought fiction of Romance?
While the dark Genius of our northern clime,
Whose giant limbs the mist of years enshrouds,

Bursts through the veil which hides his head sublime,

And moves majestic through recoiling clouds!

O yes! they own the wond'rous spell,

And to each form their hands divine

Give, with nice art, the temper'd swell,

The chasten'd touch and faultless line!

Each fiction under their command,

Assumes an air severely true,

And, every vision, wildly grand,

Life's measur'd pace and modest hue.

Reason and fancy, rival powers!

Unite, their RADCLIFFE to befriend;

To decorate her way with flowers,

The minor graces all attend!

This piece, with the exception of a few lines, has appeared in the Athenaeum.

THE HEIR.

See yon tall stripling! how he droops forlorn!

How slow his pace! how spiritless his eye!

Like a dark cloud in summer's rosy dawn,

He saddens pleasure as he passes by.

Long kept in exile by paternal pride,

He feels no joy beneath this splendid dome;

For, till the elder child of promise died,

He knew a dearer, though a humbler home.

Then the proud sail was spread! The youth obey'd,

Left ev'ry friend, and every scene he knew;

For ever left the soul-affianc'd maid,

Though his heart sicken'd as he said — Adieu;

And nurses still, with superstitious care,

The sigh of fond remembrance and despair.

TO A LLANGOLLEN ROSE,

THE DAY AFTER IT HAD BEEN GIVEN BY MISS PONSONBY.

Soft blushing flow'r! my bosom grieves,

To view thy sadly drooping leaves:

For, while their tender tints decay,

The rose of Fancy fades away!

As pilgrims, who, with zealous care,

Some little treasur'd relic bear,

To re-assure the doubtful mind,

When pausing memory looks behind;

I, from a more enlighten'd shrine,

Had made this sweet memento mine:

But, lo! its fainting head reclines;

It folds the pallid leaf, and pines,

As mourning the unhappy doom,

Which tears it from so sweet a home!

July 22, 1799.

L'HOMME DE L'ENNUI.

Forlornly I wander, forlornly I sigh,

And droop my head sadly, I cannot tell why:

When the first breeze of morning blows fresh in my face,

As the wild-waving walks of our woodlands I trace,

Reviv'd for the moment I look all around,

But my eyes soon grow languid, and fix on the ground.

I have yet no misfortune to rob me of rest,

No love discomposes the peace of my breast;

Ambition ne'er enter'd the verge of my thought,

Nor by honours, by wealth, nor by power am I caught;

Those phantoms of folly disturb not my ease,

Yet Time is a tortoise, and Life a disease.

With the blessings of youth and of health on my side,

A temper untainted by envy or pride;

No guilt to corrode, and no foes to molest;

There are many who tell me my station is blest.

This I cannot dispute; yet without knowing why —

I feel that my bosom is big with a sigh.

Oh! why do I see that all knowledge is vain;

That Science finds Error still keep in her train;

That Imposture or Darkness, with Doubt and Surmise,

Will mislead, will perplex, and then baffle the wise,

Who often, when labours have shorten'd their span,

Declare — not to know — is the province of man?

In life, as in learning, our views are confin'd,

Our discernment too weak to discover the mind,

Which, subdued and irresolute, keeps out of sight;

Or if, for a moment, her presence delight,

Our air is too gross for the stranger to stay;

And, back to her prison she hurries away!

If my own narrow precincts I seek to explore,

My wishes how vain, my attainments how poor!

Tenacious of virtue, with caution I move;

I correct, and I wrestle, but cannot approve;

Till, bewilder'd and faint, I would yield up the rein,

But I dare not in peace with my errors remain!

With zeal all awake in the cause of a friend,

With warmth unrepress'd by my fear to offend,

With sympathy active in hope or distress,

How keen and how anxious I cannot express,

I shrink, lest an eye should my feelings behold,

And my heart seems insensible, selfish and cold.

I strive to be gay, but my efforts are weak,

And, sick of existence, for pleasure I seek;

I mix with the empty, the loud, and the vain,

Partake of their folly, and double my pain.

In others I meet with depression and strife;

Oh! where shall I seek for the music of life?

THE GRANDFATHER'S DEPARTURE.

The Old Man press'd Palemon's hand;

To Lucy nodded with a smile;

Kiss'd all the little ones around;

Then clos'd the gate, and paus'd awhile.

"When shall I come again!" he thought,

Ere yet the journey had begun;

It was a tedious length of way,

But he beheld an only son.

And dearly did he love to take

A rosy grandchild on his knee;

To part his shining locks, and say,

"Just such another boy was he!"

And never felt he greater pride,

And never did he look so gay,

As when the little urchins strove

To make him partner in their play.

But when, in some more gentle mood,

They silent hung upon his arm,

Or nestled close at ev'ning pray'r,

The old man felt a softer charm;

And upward rais'd his closing eye,

Whence slow effus'd a grateful tear,

As if his senses own'd a joy,

Too holy for endurance here.

No heart e'er pray'd so fervently,

Unprompted by an earthly zeal,

None ever knew such tenderness,

That did not true devotion feel.

As with the pure, uncolour'd flame,

The violet's richest blues unite,

Do our affections soar to heav'n,

And rarify and beam with light.

REFLECTIONS

OCCASIONED BY THE DEATH OF FRIENDS.

My happiness was once a goodly tree,
Which promis'd every day to grow more fair,
And rear'd its lofty branches in the air,
In sooth, it was a pleasant sight, to see!
Amidst, fair honey-suckles crept along,
Twin'd round the bark, and hung from every bough,
While birds, which Fancy held by slender strings,
Plum'd the dark azure of their shining wings,
Or dipp'd them in the silver stream below,
With many a joyful note, and many a song!
When lo! a tempest hurtles in the sky!
Dark low'r the clouds! the thunders burst around!
Fiercely the arrowy flakes of lightning fly!
While the scar'd songsters leave the quiv'ring bough,
The blasted honey-suckles droop below,
And many noble branches strew the ground!
Though soon the air is calm, the sky serene,
Though wide the broad and leafy arms are spread,
Yet still the scars of recent wounds are seen;
Their shelter henceforth seems but insecure;
The winged tribes disdain the frequent lure,
Where many a songster lies benumb'd or dead;
And when I would the flow'ry tendrils train,

I find my late delightful labour vain.

Affection thus, once light of heart, and gay,

Chasten'd by memory, and, unnerv'd by fear,

Shall sadden each endearment with a tear,

Sorrowing the offices of love shall pay,

And scarcely dare to think that good her own,

Which fate's imperious hand may snatch away,

In the warm sunshine of meridian day,

And when her hopes are full and fairest blown.

TO MRS. T. FANCOURT,

July 15, 1803.

I love not yon gay, painted flower,

Of bold and coarsely blended dye,

But one, whose nicely varied power

May long detain the curious eye.

I love the tones that softly rise,

And in a fine accordance close;

That waken no abrupt surprise,

Nor leave us to inert repose.

I love the moon's pure, holy light,

Pour'd on the calm, sequester'd stream;

The gale, fresh from the wings of night,

Which drinks the early solar beam;

The smile of heaven, when storms subside,

When the moist clouds first break away;

The sober tints of even-tide,

Ere yet forgotten by the day.

Such sights, such sounds, my fancy please,

And set my wearied spirit free:

And one who takes delight in these,

Can never fail of loving thee!

TO A YOUNG GENTLEMAN.

July 29th, 1803.

Dear boy, when you meet with a rose,

Admire you the thorns very much?

Or like you to play with a ball,

When the handling it blisters your touch!

Yet should it be firm and compact,

It is easy to polish it nice;

If the rose is both pretty and sweet,

The thorns will come off in a trice.

The thistle has still many more,

As visible too in our eyes,

But who will take pains with a weed,

That nobody ever can prize?

'Tis what we deem precious and rare,

We most earnestly seek to amend;

And anxious attention and care,

Is the costliest gift of a friend.

We all have our follies: what then?

Let us note them, and never look bluff!

Without any caressing at all,

They will cling to us closely enough.

Weeds are of such obstinate growth,

They elude the most diligent hand;

And, if they were not to be check'd,

Would quickly run over the land.

If some could be taken away,

That hide part of your worth from the view;

The conquest perhaps would be ours,

But the profit is wholly to you.

FRAGMENT.

A Pilgrim weary, toil-subdued,

I reach'd a country, strange and rude,

And trembled, lest approaching eve

My hope of shelter might deceive;

When I espied a hunter train,

Prowling at leisure o'er the plain,

And hasten'd on to ask relief,

Of the ill-omen'd, haughty chief.

His eye was artful, keen, and bold,

His smile malevolently cold,

And had not all my fire been fled,

And every earthly passion dead,

His pity to contempt allied,

Had rous'd my anger and my pride;

But, as it was, I bent my way,

Where his secluded mansion lay,
Which rose before my eyes at length,
A fortress of determin'd strength,
And layers of every colour'd moss
The lofty turrets did emboss,
As tho' the hand of father Time,
Prepar'd a sacrifice sublime,—
Giving his daily rites away,
To aggrandize some future day.
Here as I roam'd the walk along,
I heard a plaintive broken song;
And ere I to the portal drew,
An open window caught my view,
Where a fair dame appear'd in sight,
Array'd in robes of purest white.
Large snowy folds confin'd her hair,
And left a polish'd forehead bare.
O'er her meek eyes, of deepest blue,
The sable lash long shadows threw;
Her cheek was delicately pale,
And seem'd to tell a piteous tale,
But o'er her looks such patience stole,
Such saint-like tenderness of soul,
That never did my eyes behold,
A beauty of a lovelier mold.
The Lady sigh'd, and closely prest
A sleeping infant to her breast;
Shook off sweet tears of love, and smil'd,

Kissing the fingers of the child,

Which round her own unconscious clung,

Then fondly gaz'd, and softly sung:

> Once like that sea, which ebbs and flows,
>
> My bosom never knew repose,
>
> And heavily each morn arose.
>
> I bore with anger and disdain,
>
> I had no power to break my chain,
>
> No one to whom I dar'd complain.
>
> And when some bird has caught my eye,
>
> Or distant sail been flitting by,
>
> I wish'd I could at freely fly.
>
> But I can now contented be,
>
> Can tell, dear babe, my griefs to thee.
>
> And feel more brave, and breathe more free.
>
> And when thy father frowns severe,
>
> Although my spirit faints with fear,
>
> I feel I have a comfort near.
>
> And when he harshly speaks to me,
>
> If thou art smiling on my knee,
>
> He softens as he looks on thee.
>
> To soothe him in an evil hour
>
> The bud has balm, oh! may the flower
>
> Possess the same prevailing power!
>
> Nor forc'd to leave thy native land,
>
> To pledge a cold, unwilling hand,
>
> May'st thou receive the hard command.
>
> My mother had not half the zeal,

The aching fondness which I feel,
She had no broken heart to heal!
And I was friendless when she died,
Who could my little failings chide,
And for an hour her fondness hide.
But I can see no prospect ope,
Can give no fairy vision scope,
If thou art not the spring of hope.
I cannot thy affection draw,
By childhood's first admiring awe;
Be tender pity then thy law!
This heart would bleed at every vein,
I could not even life sustain,
If ever thou should'st give me pain.
O! soul of sweetness! can it be,
That thou could'st prove unkind to me!
That I should fear this blow from thee!
Alas! e'en then I would not blame,
My love to thee should be the same,
And judge from whence unkindness came!

Her words grew indistinct and slow,
Her voice more tremulous and low,
When suddenly the song was o'er,
A whisper even heard no more —
She had discern'd my nearer tread;
Appear'd to feel alarm, and fled.

SONGS.

SONG.

Thrice lovely babe! thus hush'd to rest,
Upon thy warrior father's breast!
Avails it, that his eyes behold,
Thy rosy cheeks, thy locks of gold!
Avails it that he bends his ear,
So fondly thy soft breath to hear!
Or, that his rising smiles confess,
A gracious gleam of tenderness!
The sweetest spell will scarce have pow'r
To hold him for one absent hour!
Some plant that ceases thus to share,
A daily friend's auspicious care,
Relaxes in its feeble grasp,
The flow'ry tendrils soon unclasp,
Loose in the heedless aether play,
And every idle breeze obey!
Thus vainly had I sought to bind;
Thus watch'd that light, forgetful mind,
Till smiles and sunshine could restore,
My often-blighted hopes no more!

SONG.

SET TO MUSIC BY MR. VOIGHT.

What do I love? A polish'd mind,
A temper cheerful, meek, and kind;

A graceful air, unsway'd by art,

A voice that sinks into the heart,

A playful and benignant smile—

Alas! my heart responds the while,

All this, my Emily, is true,

But I love more in loving you!

I love those roses when they rise,

From joy, from anger, or surprise;

I love the kind, attentive zeal,

So prompt to know what others feel,

The mildness which can ne'er reprove,

But in the sweetest tones of love—

All this, my Emily, is true,

But I love more in loving you!

The self-command which can sustain,

In silence, weariness and pain;

The transport at a friend's success,

Which has not words or power to bless,

But, by a sudden, starting tear,

Appears more precious, more sincere—

All this, my Emily, is true,

And this I love in loving you!

A SAILOR'S SONG.

SET TO MUSIC BY MR. WALSH.

I ponder many a silent hour,

On friends belov'd when far at sea,

And, tell me, have I not the power
To draw one kindred thought to me!
The while we linger on the coast,
My truant fancy homeward flies,
And when the view is almost lost,
Unmanly tears bedew my eyes —
And oft forgetful do I stand,
Nor crew, nor ship, nor ocean see;
And often does my heart demand,
If friends belov'd thus think on me!
And when to England bound once more,
I shall with fond impatience burn,
Will not some others on the shore
As fondly look for my return!
O! let me of your kindness hear!
Repeat the strain as I depart!
It swells like music on my ear,
It falls like balm upon my heart.

Aug. 21, 1805.

ANOTHER,

WRITTEN EARLIER.

Adieu to old England! adieu to my friends!

Though fortune and fame I pursue,

On thus looking around me, I cannot conceal,

How reluctant I bid them adieu!

My heart sinks within me, I sigh to the gale,

Thus slowly receding from shore,

While fancy still whispers some terrible tale,

A perhaps I may see it no more!

There all that I love, that I value, remain,

That only awakens my fears,

For will the same spot its dear inmates contain,

On the lapse of two lingering years?

They may smile in good fortune, or weep in distress,

I shall know not a word of their fate!

No pain can I soften, no sorrow redress!

I may come, when, alas! 'tis too late!

I can fly without fear to encounter the foe,

To my earliest wish I am true;

But I cannot unmov'd quit the friends that I love,

Or bid my dear country adieu!

SONG.

SET TO MUSIC BY MR. A. PETTIT, OF NORWICH.

Once more then farewell! and whilst I'm away,

Oh! let not another entangle thy fancy!

I shall think upon thee every hour of the day,

And let not my love be forgotten by Nancy!

Oh! were I forsaken, the flow'r in my heart,

Would fold all its leaves, and re-open them never!

The sunshine of joy and of hope would depart,

And belief in affection would perish for ever!

To talk thus is folly! I doubt not thy truth,

A few years of absence will quickly pass over,

I scorn other perils that menace my youth,

From that wound, I must own, I could never recover!

HENRY,

ON THE DEPARTURE OF HIS WIFE FROM CALCUTTA.

Long is thy passage o'er the main,

And native air alone can save!

No friend thy weakness will sustain,

But India is, for thee, a grave!

Though winds arise, though surges swell,

Maria, we must say farewell!

Oh! I bethink me of the time,

When with each airy hope in view,

In triumph to this fervid clime

I bore a flowret nurs'd in dew!

No fears did then my joy reprove,

And it was boundless as my love!

Yet now to strangers I consign

Thy wounded mind, thy feeble health;

A charge more dear than life resign,

To watch a little worldly wealth.

Duty compels me to remain

But oh! how heavy feels the chain!

My dear Maria! smile no more?

This seeming patience makes me wild!

So would'st thou once my peace restore,

When, mourning for our only child,

Each faint appeal was lost in air,

Or turn'd my sadness to despair.

Alas! I only make thee grieve.

And hark! the boat awaits below!

They call aloud! and I must leave,

The tears my folly forc'd to flow.

Oh! had I but the time to prove,

That mine are only fears of love!

SONNET.

Urge me no more! nor think, because I seem

Tame and unsorrowing in the world's rude strife,

That anguish and resentment have not life

Within the heart that ye so quiet deem:

In this forc'd stillness only, I sustain

My thought and feeling, wearied out with pain!

Floating as 'twere upon some wild abyss,

Whence, silent Patience, bending o'er the brink,

Would rescue them with strong and steady hand,
And join again, by that connecting link,
Which now is broken:—O, respect her care!
Respect her in this fearful self-command!
No moment teems with greater woe than this,
Should she but pause, or falter in despair!

ON THE REGRET OF YOUTH.

Before a rose is fully blown,
The outward leaves announce decay;
So, ere the spring of Youth is flown,
Its tiny pleasures die away;
The gay security we feel,
The careless soul's delighted rest,
That lively hope, that ardent zeal,
And smiling sunshine of the breast.
Those simple tints, so bright and clear,
No healing dew-drops can restore;
For joys, which early life endear,
Once blighted, can revive no more.
Yet lovely is the full-blown rose,
Although its infant graces fly;
The various opening leaves disclose,
A fairer banquet to the eye;
A ruby's beams on drifted snow,
Such pure, harmonious blushes shed;
If distant, cast a tender glow,
But near, its own imperial red;

The form assumes a prouder air,

And bends more graceful in the gale;

While, from its cup, of essence rare,

A richer hoard of sweets exhale.

Could we again, by fancy led,

That bower of swelling leaves confine,

And round that fine, luxuriant head,

The mossy tendrils now entwine,

Over what multitudes of bloom

Would a few timid leaflets close!

What mental joys resign their room,

To causeless mirth, and tame repose!

The change to Reason's steady eye,

Would neither good nor wise appear;

And we may lay one precept by,

Our discontent is insincere.

ELEGY ON SOPHIA GRAHAM,

WHO DIED JAN. 21, 1800.

Sweet is the voice of Friendship to the ear,

Sweet is Affection's mildly-beaming eye,

Sweet the applause which flows from lips sincere,

And sweet is Pity's soft responsive sigh!

But now those flowers of life have lost their bloom,

Faint all their beauty, cold their healing breath,

No object fills my eye but yonder tomb,

No sound awakes me but the name of death.

When in the world, I bear a look serene,
And veil the gloomy temper of my grief;
Sick with restraint at evening quit the scene,
To find in tears and solitude relief.
Parent of Hope and Fancy! thoughtful Night!
Why are these nurselings absent from thy bower,
While Memory, with sullen, strange delight,
Stalks lonely centinel the live-long hour?
O dear Sophia! could we e'er forget,
Such fair endowments and unsullied worth,
Thy partial friendship calls for our regret,
And selfish feeling gives remembrance birth.
How often when this trembling hand essays
Thy lov'd resemblance once again to trace,
The portrait thought in mimic life arrays
With all the sweet expression of thy face;
Art may its symmetry and beauty show,
A look, a character, the pencil seize,
Give to the form where youthful graces glow,
An air of pensive dignity and ease,
But warmth of feeling and sensation fine,
By mild reserve from common eyes conceal'd,
The ray of genius and the heart benign,
In artless gaiety so oft reveal'd —
All these are lost; no looks can now arise,
Like those which every little act endear'd,
Which even in the stranger's careless eyes
Like innocence from other worlds appear'd!

Oft have I fear'd the breath of foolish praise,

Might taint the lily which so humbly grew;

That flattery's sun might shoot delusive rays,

Impede her progress, and distract her view.

But vain the fear—for she remain'd the same,

To outward charms indifferent or blind,

Heedless alike of either praise or blame,

If it respected not her heart and mind.

Rich in historic lore, the poet's lyre

Had not, though screen'd by time, forsaken hung,

She felt and studied with a kindred fire,

The lofty strain immortal Maro sung.

She knew—but why essay to trace her thought

Through its wide range, describe her blooming youth,

The heart whose feelings were so finely wrought,

Its meek ambition, and its love of truth?

All that parental-vanity desires,

All that the friend can muse upon and mourn,

All that the lover's ardent vow inspires,

In thee, Sophia! from the world was torn!

But still we yield thee to no stranger's care;

No unknown foe our tender love bereaves;

Thou goest the angels' hallow'd bliss to share,

A Father thy exalted soul receives!

TO MISS ROUSE BOUGHTON,

NOW THE RIGHT HON. LADY ST. JOHN.

Aberystwith, July 5th, 17 —

Louisa, while thy pliant fingers trace

The solemn beauties of the prospect round,

Or, on thy instrument, with touching grace,

Awaken all the witcheries of sound:

Mild, as thy manners, do the colours rise,

As soft and unobtrusive meet the view;

And, when the varied notes the ear surprize,

We own the harmony as strictly true.

Be thine the praise, alas! a gift how rare!

Artless, and unpretending, to excel!

Forget the envied charm of being fair,

To learn the noblest science, — acting well!

And let no world the seal of truth displace,

Or spoil the heart's accordance with the face!

TO THE SAME,

ON RECEIVING FROM HER A FEW FLOWERS OUT OF A BOUQUET, FROM MELCHBOURNE, 1807.

Hail! sweet Louisa! o'er these votive flow'rs

Friendship and Fancy weave the joyful song,

Wing with fresh rose-leaves all the train of hours,

That in the distant aether float along!

Like those fair flowrets given by thy hand,

Like thy own beauty, blooming and serene,

The vision of thy future life is plann'd,

And forms a clear, a bright, and varied scene!

That countenance so gentle, and so kind,

That heart, which never gave a harsh decree,

Suit all the turns of thy harmonious mind,

And must, perforce, with destiny agree.

This from the Sibyl's leaves affection drew,

O, be the omen just! the promise true!

TO THE RIVER

WHICH SEPARATES ITSELF FROM THE DEE, AT BEDKEL-LERT.

July 19, 1799.

Let others hail the tranquil stream,

Whose glassy waters smoothly flow,

And, in the undulating gleam,

Reflect another world below!

The yellow Conway as it raves,

Demands my tributary song!

When, rushing forth, resistless waves

O'er rocky fragments foam along!

Like him, whose vigorous mind reviews

The troubles which around him roll;

The ceaseless warfare still pursues,

And keeps a firm, undaunted soul.

Though sternly bent by toil and care,

The brow hang darkly o'er his eye —

His features the fix'd meaning wear
Of one who knows not how to sigh.
It is not apathy that reigns,
O'erweening arrogance, or pride,
For, in his warmly-flowing veins,
The genial feelings all reside.
It is the breast-plate fortitude
Should still to injury oppose;
It is the shield with power imbu'd,
To blunt the malice of his foes.
And should the savage country round,
A more engaging aspect show,
O Conway! it will then be found,
How sweet and clear thy waters flow!
The birds will dip the taper wing—
The pilgrim there his thirst assuage,
The wandering minstrel sit and sing,
Or muse upon a distant age!
Bold River! soon within the deep,
Each weary strife and conflict o'er,
Thy venerable waves shall sleep,
And feel opposing rocks no more!

THE OLD MAN'S FAREWELL.

Farewell, my pilgrim guest, farewell,
A few days since thou wert unknown,
None shall thy future fortunes tell,
But sweetly have the moments flown!

And kindness, like the sun on flowers,

Soon chas'd away thy tender gloom;

New-fledg'd the sable-pinion'd hours,

And wove bright tints in Fancy's loom.

We sought no secrets to divine,

Neither thy name nor lineage knew,

Our hearts alone have question'd thine,

And found that all was just and true.

Pass not with hasty step, I pray,

Across the threshold of my door!

But pause awhile, with kind delay,

We shall behold thy face no more!

Once only in a hundred years,

The aloe's precious blossoms swell,

So, in thy presence it appears,

That Time has blossom'd, fare thee well! *

Footnote: See Preface. (return)

SONG.

DISTANCE FROM THE PLACE OF OUR NATIVITY.

Since I married Palemon, though happy my lot,

Though my garden is pleasant, and lightsome my cot,

Though love's smile, like a sunshine, I constantly see,

Those blessings are all insufficient for me,

I repine not at labour, I ask not for gold,

But I want the sweet eyes of my friends to behold.

With Palemon I think o'er the world I could roam,

Though he liv'd in a desert, would make it my home.

From him no allurements his Lucy could bribe,

And, though timid, no dangers, no menaces drive.

But the heart that can love with devotion so true,

Is not cold or forgetful, my parents, to you!

Oh idle declaimers! how is it ye say,

That affection and tenderness fade and decay?

Though so easily pain'd, they endure like a gem,

And the heart and the mind imbibe colour from them!

In affliction they brighten, in absence refine,

And are causes of sorrow too sweet to resign.

THE OLD SHEPHERD'S RECOLLECTIONS.

Low, heavy clouds are hanging on the hills,

And half-impatient of the sun's approach,

Shake sullenly their cold and languid wings!

Oh! it is fine to see his morning beams

Burst on the gloom, while, in disorder'd flight,

The shuddering, mournful vapours steal away;

Like the tenacious spirit of a man,

Shrinking from the loud voice of cheerfulness,

When it breaks in, so sadly out of tune,

Upon his quiet musing, and dispels

The waking dream of a dejected heart:

The dream I cherish in this solitude,

In all the wanderings of my little flock,

That which beguiles my loneliness, and takes

Its charm and change from the surrounding scene.

Oh! how unwelcome often are to me

The gayest, most exhilarating sounds!

When slow and sickly Memory, tempted forth

By dint of soft persuasion, brings to light

His treasures—and, with childish eagerness,

Arranges and collects—then suddenly

To have him startled by discordance, drag,

Without discrimination, all away—

And with them leap to his deep hollow cave—

Not easily to be withdrawn again,

Grieves one who loves to think of other times,

To talk with those long silent in the grave,

And pass from childhood to old age again.

Behold this stony rock! whose rifted crest,

Lets the rough, roaring torrent force a way,

And, foaming, pour its waters on the vale!

Behold them tumbling from their dizzy height,

Like clouds, of more than snowy whiteness, thrown

Precipitate from heav'n, which, as they fall,

Diffuse a mist, in form of glory, round!

This was my darling haunt a long time past!

Here, when a boy, in pleasing awe, I sate,

Wistfully silent, with uplifted eye,

And heart attun'd to the sad, lulling sound

They made descending. Far below my feet,

Near where yon little, ruin'd cottage lies,

Oft, at the pensive hour of even-tide

I saw young Osborne bearing on his harp,

And, trusting to an aged mother's care,

His darkling steps: Beneath that falling beech,

Whose wide-spread branches touch the water's edge,

He lov'd to sit, and feel the freshen'd gale

Breathe cool upon him. Then that falling beech

Was a young, graceful tree; which, starting up,

Amid the looser fragments of the rock,

Rear'd boldly in the air its lofty head,

While, struggling with the stone, the nervous roots

Pursued their own direction, elbowing out,

Their flinty neighbour; who, o'erspread with moss,

Of varied hues, and deck'd with flow'ring heath,

That from each fissure hung luxuriant down,

Became a seat, where, king of all the scene,

The harper sate, and, in sweet melodies,

Now like the lark rejoicing at the dawn,

Now soothing as the nightingale's sad note,

Hail'd the departing sun, whose golden rays

Glitter'd upon the surface of the wave,

And, as a child upon its mother's arm

Seeks to delay the coming hour of rest,

Till sudden slumbers steal upon his smiles

And veil him in a dream of love and joy,

He seem'd reluctant to withdraw his beams;

And, rich in roseate beauty, for awhile

Kept the green waves beneath his glowing head.

Kind, gentle Osborne! half a century

Has silver'd o'er the crisp and yellow locks

Of thy young auditor, but memory still

Grasps the torn record of my weary life.

And finds full many a page to tell of thee!

Oh! ye who have a friend ye truly love,

One whom your hearts can trust, whose excellence

Was not obtruded boastingly to view,

But time and happy circumstance reveal'd,

Rays of quick light upon a diamond

Which else had lain unnotic'd in the waste!

Oh! hasten! hasten speedily to pay

Each debt of fond affection! lock not up

So cautiously the tribute due to worth!

Nor let reserve, as I have often done,

Enslave the sweetest feelings of the soul!

And hang around them like an envious mist,

O'er the bright radiance of the morning star,

Leaving us nothing but a spot of light

Bereav'd of all its lustre! For my friend,

He never knew that there was one on earth,

After a parent felt the touch of death,

And Love, a weeping pilgrim, turn'd away

Far from his dwelling—Oh! he never knew,

That there was one who would have follow'd him,

With steady kindness, even to the grave!

Thou dear, neglected friend! to whom I owe

All that sustains my heart, and makes me think

The gift of life a blessing, Oh! forgive

That in thy sorrows, my forgetful tongue

Spake not of zeal and service; of the debt
Which gratitude was emulous to pay!
I might have trimm'd the dying lamp of hope,
And cheer'd the bitter hours of banishment:
But Oh! my youth was fearful, and I felt
So deep an awe of that unspotted worth
And saint-like gentleness — such a mistrust
Of my own powers to tell him what I wish'd,
That I resisted all my feelings claim'd,
In anguish I resisted; but a spell
Hung o'er me and compell'd me to be mute.
Methinks I still behold him! tall and fair,
He had a look so tranquil and so mild,
That something holy stole upon the sense
When he appear'd; his language had such power
In converse, that the hearer, as entranced
Sate lingering on to listen; while in song,
Or skill upon the many-stringed harp
Was never heard his equal! Then he knew
All our old ballads, all our father's tales,
All the adventurous deeds of early times,
The punishment of blood or sacrilege,
And the reward of virtue, when it seem'd
Deserted by the world, and left alone,
A prey to scorn, oppression, contumely
And all the ills which make the good despair.
When-e'er we circled round him, one young girl
Was always present, of a nicer ear,

And more refin'd perception than the rest.
Now she was lost in thought, while on her cheek
Lay silent tears — and then that cheek grew pale
In wild amazement — but, when he began
To speak of noble deeds, she rais'd her head,
Bending with looks of mingled awe and love,
And zealous admiration, on the youth,
Alone insensible of all around,
To the soft charm of symmetry and grace,
The smile intelligent, the look benign,
And all the outward raiment of the soul.
Yet, though he saw her not, it was his fate
To have an inward and discerning sense,
Which spake of Lora's gentleness and worth.
He lov'd in her the fondness of his art,
And taught her many wild and simple airs,
Suiting the plaintive tenor of her voice,
Which he would mimic with sweet minstrelsy.
When she was absent, and with strange delight,
Repeat her parting words, her kind adieu,
Or sweetly-spoken promise of return.
And that return was prompt: she linger'd oft
Till evening wet the ground with heavy dew,
Or came to take her lesson in the morn,
Before her father's anxious eyes unclos'd,
To look upon her beauty with delight,
And soothe the rugged temper of his soul,
By views of future grandeur for his child:

Not thinking that her elegance of mind,
The modest dignity of humble worth
Which fits the low-born peasant to become
A crowned monarch, and to wield with grace
The golden sceptre, had instructed her
To feel no paltry jealousy of power,
No bold aspiring, and no wish beyond
The bounded confines of her present state:
Had counsell'd her, that even mines of wealth,
Could purchase nothing to content the wise,
Esteem or friendship, tenderness or love:
That power at best was but a heavy weight;
If well employ'd, a dubious, unpaid toil,
If ill, a curse, to tempt men to their fate.
Her cheek had often felt the blush of shame,
At his proud boasting; and her heart had sunk
At the cold arrogance that scorn'd the poor;
But she was fain to turn aside, and weep,
To wring her hands in secret, and to raise
The eye of silent anguish up to heaven;
For though he dearly lov'd her, he would ne'er
Submit to hear a murmur at his will.
Oft with her heart oppress'd, and her blue eyes
Full of unshedden tears, she bent her way
Alone to Osborne's lowly cot, and when
Her faint voice call'd the fond inquiry forth,
Would say, "'tis true, my friends, that I am sad,
Nay sick, with vain repining. O! I wish,

That I were either indigent myself,

Or that I had the power, the blessed power

Of cheering the unhappy! for I want,

By kindness to prevent the act of guilt,

And ward the arrows of incroaching Death,

Who comes, before the time, upon his prey.

Think that there should be means to stay his wrath,

To purchase health, life, comfort, innocence,

And yet those means withholden! "O! my heart!

It dies with sorrow! and where most I love,

Sheds all its bitterness; delighting still

To tell the many miseries that flit

At times across me! Those I lightly prize

Partake the sunshine of my happier hours,

Although I seek them with far less delight!

The loud laugh dwells not here, the sportive dance,

The carol of unconscious levity,

And yet how oft, how willingly I come!"

"Know'st thou not, Lora," cried the youthful sage,

"That there are things the mind must prize above

What captivates the senses! That in them

She feels no interest, and she takes no care!

That though sometimes an alien, she receives

Delighted back the ensigns of her power,

And takes her truant vassals into grace!

That when thou bring'st to us that wounded mind,

The grave of many feelings, language is

As yet too poor to utter, thou canst give

No richer, dearer token of regard."

"Were man indeed the only hope of man,

I never would reprove thee for thy tears!

But, they are vain! man has a surer trust!

The helpless, weary, miserable wretch,

Left by his fellows in the wilderness,

Shall be supported in that trying hour,

By a right arm, which, in his days of strength,

He did not lean upon! A gracious arm,

Which wounds the sick, and heals them by the stroke.

O! Lora! to the Father of the world,

A Judge so patient and so merciful.

That he refuses not the latest sigh.

Nor suffers sorrow but as means to save,

Canst thou not trust the objects of thy care!

"Hadst thou the power to help them—it were well,

To be most anxious. To collect thy freight

Of human sorrow, and, by merchandize,

Exchange it for the riches of the world:

For health, for comfort, nay, perchance for life,

That gem of countless value, which sometimes,

Not all the treasures of the East can buy,

Tendered with supplications and with tears,

Is often purchas'd at a petty price,

Nay, in exchange for courtesy. What joy

Must in that moment fill the merchant's heart,

To win a jewel, kings monopolize

The sole disposal of! Be patient then!

This glorious privilege may yet be thine!
Deserve it only by fulfilling all
The gentler duties that have present claims
With cheerfulness and zeal—Let no neglect
Press on thy father's age, no discontent
Sour thee with thy companions, no mistrust
Give pain to friendship, and thy usefulness
Though calm and bounded, has no mean award."
Thus, like a prophet, did he still enforce
Only the virtues and rare qualities
Congenial with her after destiny;
Yet, not foreseeing evil, he himself
Was unprepared, and when her father led,
Her opposition and entreaty past,
The hapless Lora forth, to promise love
And honour to a man, whose vacant mind,
Throughout a course of long succeeding years,
She vainly strove to soften and to raise,
Though he had taught her patience till that hour,
His own at once forsook him, and he fled.
She murmur'd not, nor even seem'd to mourn,
But losing all her love of solitude,
Appear'd so active in each new pursuit,
So wholly what her anxious father wish'd,
That he repented not his cruelty.
Believing in her happiness, he felt
Himself the author, and became more proud
Of his own wisdom: yet she often heard

His wayward taunt or querulous complaint,
And, from the lordly partner of her fate,
The harsher sound of ignorant rebuke.
She was a matchless woman, when she lost
The timid graces of retiring youth,
She still was lovely, for her shaded eyes
Beam'd with a lofty sweetness, a content
Beyond the pow'r of fortune to destroy.
Careless of let or hindrance, she went on,
Nor shrunk nor started at the many thorns
Strew'd in her toilsome path; still looking forth
To others' weal, forgetful it would seem,
Perchance in heart despairing of her own.
The friend, the help, the comforter of all,
No voice was heard so cheerful, nor a step
So bounding and so light. 'Twas wonderful!
For I have seen her, when her polish'd arm
Has clasp'd the nurseling, with her face conceal'd
Bent fondly o'er; and I have mark'd each limb
To boast a fine expansion, as if thrill'd
With the deep feelings of maternal love
And aching tenderness, too highly wrought
For happy souls to cherish! they delight
In painless joys, and, on the infant's cheek,
Rounded and glowing with a finer bloom
Than the wild-rose, careless imprint the kiss,
Which sorrow always sanctions by a prayer.
They in the radiance of its glancing eyes

See nothing to suffuse with their own tears!
Borne forward on the easy wing of Time,
They travel on, they scarcely meet with Thought,
Or, like a summer cloud, he passes by,
His shadow rests one instant, and again
The scene is calm and brilliant as before!
Not so with Lora, trouble, sickness, death,
Were busy with the residue of peace,
When years and care had weaken'd her regrets,
Veil'd the sad recollection of past days,
And overgrown the softness of her mind,
As the close-creeping ivy hides and rusts
The smooth and silver surface of the beech.
An orphan and a widow — she became
Decisive, watchful, prudent, nay severe
To wilful disobedience or neglect;
Though generous where she perceiv'd desert.
She taught her children with unceasing zeal,
Sought knowledge for their sakes, and, more than all,
Anxious, inquisitive about the heart,
Search'd all the motives, all the incidents
In which it was unfolded; fencing still
Each treacherous failing with a double guard,
And oft repeated warnings; well conceal'd,
Or given with so much kindness, that they serv'd
To draw more closely every knot of love.
Nor did she cease to urge her pious cares
By constant vigilance, till riper age

Had fix'd the moral sense, when, as a bow

For a long active season tightly strain'd

Relaxes, tumult and contention o'er,

She sunk into indulgence, glad to yield

To mildness, nature, and herself again.

Youth, e'en when wise and good, requires a change,

Delights in novelty, and hears of nought

Which suddenly it asks not to behold;

And Lora's children oft assail'd her ear

To let them journey to some rumour'd scene,

Some feast, or village wake, or sprightly dance,

Urging her still to bear them company.

She lov'd to give them pleasure, and one time

(The fav'rite legend of our country folk

Hath oft the tale repeated) as they mix'd

Carelessly in the crowd, remember'd notes

Struck by a harper in a distant tent,

Sweet and soul-piercing as the midnight songs

Which are, they say, the harbingers of death,

Flow'd on her ear—when, with impulsive spring,

As if a magic spell had wing'd her feet,

Fearing the sounds would vanish into air,

And prove delusion ere she reach'd the spot,

She forward rush'd, and soon beheld the friend,

The dear companion of her youth. She seiz'd

The hand that lay upon the quivering chords,

Stopping their melody and resting mute.

The pause was awful—He at length exclaim'd,

In a deep, laboured cry, "Ye heavenly powers!

If Lora lives, the hand I feel is hers!"

She could not speak, but with her other hand

Clasp'd his, and sigh'd and rais'd her eyes to heaven,

When straight the big, round tears began to flow;

"And is it thee, dear Lora! Art thou come

Again to gladden one, who never found

'Mid countless who are good, a heart like thine!

Oh! speak! that I may know if still my ear

Retains a true remembrance of that voice!

For since, it has not drank so sweet a sound."

"Hail happy day!" cried Lora, "which restores

The friend whose absence I have mourn'd so long!

For thou, O! Osborne! must with me return,

Me and my children! They shall hear again

Those counsels which inform'd their mother's heart;

Gave courage in the hour of enterprize,

Calmness in danger, patience under ills

That like a swarm of insects buz around,

And vex the spirit which they cannot rouse.

Return, my early, long-lost friend! with us

Thou shalt enjoy repose: our cheerful home

Shall gather round thee many an honest heart

Which knows thy virtues, and will hold thee dear."

She paus'd, and Osborne joyful gave assent.

Fair hopes of joy engaged his faultering mind,

For long-time had he dragg'd a weary life,

Lone, or bereav'd of relative or friend,

Careful to tend his health, and to divert

His sadness; each succeeding hour had press'd

With its slow-passing wing his gentle head

Drooping and prematurely silver'd o'er,

(Like snows depending on the autumn leaf)

Yet warm, benevolent, serene, resign'd,

And like an angel save in youth and joy.

A winding path round yonder wooded hill,

Leads to a spot where Nature decks herself

In loveliness and beauty: far below

Spreads the green valley, where a silent stream

Turns, like a serpent writhing in its course;

And, rarified by distance, kissing heaven,

In many noble and fantastic shapes,

A giant range of purple mountains sleeps.

Grand is the scene, and in the centre stands

The tomb of Osborne—after many years

Of happiness and friendship, Lora rais'd

This plain memorial, and her children plac'd

A mother's near, to tell succeeding years

Their talents and their virtue. They themselves

More forcibly express the worth of both,

For they are wise and good, without a shade

Of cold severity or selfish pride.

REFLECTION.

August 2, 1798.

Why should we think the years of life
Will pass serenely by,
When, for a day, the Sun himself
Ne'er sees a cloudless sky!
And, unassuming as she moves,
The meek-eyed Queen of night,
Meets wand'ring vapours in her path
To dim her paler light!
Then why should we in vain repine
At man's uncertain lot,
That cares will equally assail
The palace and the cot?
For Heaven ordains this chequer'd scene
Our mortal pow'rs t' employ;
That we might know, compare, select,
Be grateful, and enjoy.

[For the last verse I am indebted to the pen of a Friend.]

RETROSPECT OF YOUTH.

I wander'd forth amid the flow'rs,
And careless sipp'd the morning air;
Nor hail'd the angel-winged hours,
Nor saw that Happiness was there!
Alas! I often since have wept
That Gratitude unconscious slept!
For Truth and Pity then were young,
And walk'd in simple, narrow bounds;

Affection's meek, assuasive tongue,

Had sweet, but most capricious sounds.

Once, wild with scornful pride, she fled,

And only turn'd to seek the dead!

Oh! from a garden of delight,

What fair memento did I bring!

What amaranth of colours bright,

To mark the promise of my spring?

Behold this flow'r! its leaves are wet,

With tears of lasting, vain regret!

THE DAUGHTER.

1797.

"Come, mournful lute! dear echo of my woe!

No stranger's tread in this lone spot I fear,

Sweeter thy notes in such wild places flow,

And, what is more, my Henry cannot hear!

"He will not know my pain and my despair,

When that dread scene arises on my view,

Where my poor father would not hear my pray'r,

Or grant his only child a last adieu!

"He will not know that still the hour I mourn,

When death all hopes of pardon snatch'd away;

That still this heart by sad remembrance torn,

Repeats the dreadful mandate of that day.

"Luckless for him has been my constant love,

Luckless the destiny I bade him brave,

For since a parent did our vows reprove,

Sorrow was all the gift my fondness gave.

"Then, though I knew my father's stern command,

The short-liv'd conflict of affection o'er,

I offer'd to the youth my dowerless hand,

And fondly reason'd thus on being poor,

"'Can pomp or splendour elevate the soul,

Brighten the lustre that illumes the eye!

Make the rough stream of life more smoothly roll,

Suppress the tear, or waft away the sigh!

"'Can happiness a purer joy receive,

In the proud mansions of the rich and great?

Or, tell me, can the wounded bosom heave

With blunted anguish under robes of state!

"'No! Henry, no! Alas! too well you know,

The misery of an affected smile,

The pain of clearing the thought-clouded brow,

To covet for yourself the hateful toil!

"'And since my choice, and reason both approve,

Since I have known you many a circling year,

And time has well assur'd me of your love,

Tell me, my Henry, what have I to fear?

"'My father, though by worldly prudence led,

Will pardon when our happiness is told.'

Alas! no curses fell upon my head,

But never did he more his child behold.

"He would not, dying, hear my ardent prayer!

But, cruel! said, I leave her all my store;

She wrung my doating heart with deep despair,

And even now perhaps desires no more.

"This is the stroke which all my peace destroys,

The dagger which no art can draw away,

The thought which every faculty employs,

Withers my bloom, and makes my strength decay.

"His death, his sorrows are the heavy curse

That hangs above my poor, distracted head!

His dying words have scatter'd vain remorse,

For vain, though bitter, are the tears I shed.

"And yet my father to my soul was dear,

But tender pity was on Henry's side;

I painted him relenting, not severe,

Nor fancied I could be an orphan bride.

"Ah me! excuses will not cure my pain!

At least, forgetfulness can little plead.

A widow'd parent!—I deserv'd disdain,

'Tis fit these eyes should weep, this heart should bleed!

"But yet assist me heaven! to hide my grief,

My waning health from love's suspicious eyes!

This malady admits of no relief,

And nought augments the pain, but Henry's sighs.

"Perhaps e'en now he wonders at my stay,

Sees the white fogs of evening rise around,

Comes out to seek me in my devious way,

But turns not to this unfrequented ground.

"Alas! my love, thy anxious care is vain!

Nothing can stop yon wand'rer of the sky;

Nothing can long this fleeting life retain!

For oh! I feel that I must shortly die.

"But cease my lute, this low, desponding strain,

It floats too long upon the heavy air;

Henry may pass and know that I complain.

One moment's peace to him is worth my care."

She said, and toward the cheerless mansion flew,

Her slender, sylph-like form array'd in white,

Not clearly seen amidst surrounding dew,

Seem'd like a spirit ling'ring in its flight.

Poor Henry, who had watch'd her in the shade,

In aching silence list'ning to her song,

At distance follow'd slowly through the glade,

Pausing forgetful as he pass'd along.

YOUTH UNSUSPICIOUS OF EVIL.

O bend thy head, sweet morning flow'r!

And look not up so fresh and bright!

The keen, harsh wind, the heavy show'r,

Will spoil thy beauties ere the night.

I grieve to see thee look so gay.

And so unconscious of thy lot,

For gloom and tempests wait thy day,

And thou, unhappy, fear'st it not!

Thy tender leaflets all unfold,

Their colours ripen and refine,

Become most lovely to behold,

And, ah! most apt to shrink and pine.

Then, bend thy head, sweet morning flow'r!

I grieve to see thee look so gay!

Close thy soft wings against the show'r,

And wait a more auspicious day!

THE MOTHER.

"And beats my heart again with joy!

And dances now my spirit light!

The skiff that holds my darling boy

This moment burst upon my sight!

"Not yet distinctly I perceive

Amid the crew his well-known form,

But still his safety I believe,

I know he has escap'd the storm.

"I feel as if my heart had wings,

And tender from excess of bliss,

His form, which airy fancy brings,

In fond emotion seem to kiss.

"Welcome the wild, imperfect rest,

Which these bewilder'd spirits share!

Welcome this tumult of the breast,

After the shudder of despair!

"My Robert he is brave and strong,

He will these flowing tears reprove.

Alas! how little know the young,

The tremor of a Mother's love.

"For we are weak from many a care,

From many a sleepless, anxious hour,

When fear and hope the bosom tear,

And ride the brain with fevering power.

"But lo! he cheerly waves his hand!

I hear his voice! I see his face!

And eager now he springs to land,

To meet a Mother's fond embrace!

"This failing heart! but joy to me,

If heaven in pity is thy guard;

And of the pangs I feel for thee,

Protection be the dear reward!"

EDGAR AND ELLEN.

"Arrest thy steps! On these sad plains,

Fair dame, no farther go!

But listen to the martial strains,

Whose wildness speaks of woe!

Hark! strife is forward on the field,

I hear the trumpet's bray!

Now spear to spear, and shield to shield,

Decides the dreadful day!

Unfit for thee, oh! Lady fair!

The scenes where men engage;

Thy gentle spirit could not bear

The fearful battle's rage."

"I prithee, stranger, let me fly!

Though pallid is my cheek,

The lightning's flash delights my eye,

I love the thunder's break.

And oft beneath our castle tow'rs,

When tempests rush'd along,

My steady hand has painted flowers,

Or voice has rais'd the song."

"Oh Lady! that bewilder'd eye

Is red with recent tears;

Already that heart-startling sigh

Proclaims thy anxious fears.

Then let a stranger's words prevail,

Nor thus in danger roam!

Here many frightful ills assail,

But safety is at home!"

"No, in some peasant's lowly cot

Perhaps she may abide,

To consecrate the humble spot,

But not where I reside.

In Hubert's halls, my father's foe,

From childhood have I dwelt,

And for his wily murderer too,

A filial fondness felt.

Ah me! how often have I press'd

The lips which seal'd his doom!

How oft the cruel hand caress'd

Which sent him to the tomb!

My nurse reveal'd the dreadful truth,

And, as she told the tale,

A sickly blight pass'd o'er my youth,

And turn'd its roses pale.

The heavy secret on my heart

Like deadly poison prey'd;

For she forbade me to impart

A word of what she said.

I, who so blithely sung before,

So peacefully had slept,

Fancied gaunt murder at the door,

And listen'd, shook, and wept.

No longer with an open smile,

I greeted all around;

My fearful looks were fix'd the while,

In terror on the ground.

All saw the change, and kindly strove

My sadness to relieve;

Base Hubert feign'd a parent's love,

Which could not see me grieve.

A painful anger flush'd my cheek,

My lip indignant smil'd,

I cried, "And did he e'er bespeak

Thy friendship for his child?"

"Ellen! when death was drawing nigh,

Thou wert his only care;

Oh! guard her, Hubert, if I die,

It is my latest prayer.

To none, dear friend, but thee," he cried,

"Whose love and truth are known,

Could I this precious charge confide,

To cherish, as thy own!"
I pledg'd my honour, to fulfil
My dearest friend's desire!
And I have ever acted still,
As honour's laws require!
Thy mind, dear Ellen, is the proof
Of my paternal care,
Since form'd beneath this friendly roof,
So excellent and fair.
Then why that cloud upon thy brow,
That sullen, fearful sigh!
That something which we must not know,
That cold and altered eye?
Why must thy proud, suspicious air,
Give every heart a pain?
Why must my son, my Edgar bear
Unmerited disdain?"
I hung my bead, my fault'ring tongue
In feeble murmurs spoke,
His specious art my bosom wrung,
I shudder'd at his look.
And thus, bewildered with my woes,
I faint and careless rove;
For oh! I cannot dwell with those
I must no longer love."
"Fair lady, calm that anxious heart,
And to my voice attend!
Thy father died by Hubert's dart,

And yet he was his friend.

For Lancaster Sir Philip rose,
And many a Yorkist slew;
Till, singling him amidst his foes,
Lord Hubert's arrow flew.

But soon we saw the victor stand
Beside, in sorrow drown'd;
And soon Sir Philip took the hand,
Which gave the deadly wound.

"My friend, unweeting was thy aim,
And is by me forgiv'n,
But oh! one sacred oath I claim,
In sight of men, and heav'n!

Oh! promise with a father's zeal,
My Ellen to protect!
Nor let her like an orphan feel
Dependence, and neglect!

And then, almost without regret,
I can my charge resign;
For, during life, I never met
So true a heart as thine."

Lord Hubert pledg'd his sacred word,
He wept, and, kneeling, swore,
In England ne'er to wield a sword,
Or shoot an arrow more.

From civil war, whose daily crimes
This island long shall rue,
From all the evil of the times,

In anguish he withdrew.

I wonder that, by nature bold,

He stoop'd to wear disguise,

Or leave the hapless tale untold,

Which wakens thy surprise!

Yet the sad shame that fill'd his breast,

May well thy pity crave,

A turtle dove may build her nest

Upon thy father's grave—"

"Stranger, that warrior from the east,

Who comes with headlong speed,

Is Edgar, Hubert's son, at least,

He rides on Edgar's steed!"

"Be calm, fair maid! Thou gallant knight,

Who speedest o'er the plain,

Give us some tidings of the fight,

The victor and the slain!

One moment stay! for many a care

Now fills us with alarm!

Is Edward King? Is Hubert's heir,

Escap'd from death and harm?"

"The sun of Lancaster is set,

And never more to rise;"

Return'd the knight, "I know not yet

If Edgar lives or dies!"

And scarce he check'd the flowing rein,

In hurried accents spoke,

And, dull and hollow was the strain

That through the helmet broke.

"Where is he?" shriek'd fair Ellen forth,

He started at the sound,

And, leaping sudden on the earth,

His armour rang around.

"Queen of my destiny!" he cried,

"Thy faithful Edgar see!

Whose welfare thou canst best decide,

For it depends on thee!

I sav'd our youthful Monarch's life,

Whose bounteous hand accords,

A dower to grace the noblest wife

That England's realm affords.

With thee his splendid gifts I share,

Or soon this youthful head

A solemn monk's dark cowl shall wear,

To love and glory dead.

Perhaps that tear upon thy cheek

Foretels a milder doom!

Thou wilt again our mansion seek,

Oh! let me lead thee home!"

FINIS.